I0601211

tight.

Syren Nightshade

Disclaimers

This story is a work of fiction. Names, characters, places, and incidents are the product of the author's imagination and/or are used fictitiously. Any resemblance to actual events, locales, or persons, living or dead, is completely coincidental.

Copyright © 2025 by Syren Nightshade

The reproduction, scanning, uploading, printing, and distribution of this story without the author's permission is a theft of the author's intellectual property.

For anyone who has ever wanted to get fucked by their sleep paralysis demon

(I hope the three of you find each other)

Content Advisory

This erotic horror story involves sexual scenes in which the narrator is cognizant of what is happening to her, but is unable to move or physically react. This content may be uncomfortable or triggering to some readers.

Please use discretion when choosing to engage with this story. Your safety is more important than reading, enjoying, or finishing this book.

PART I

I am going to die.

That's how it always starts. A tap on the shoulder. A polite whisper in the back of my mind. *Your shirt tag is out. There's sauce on your chin. You're going to die.*

And then it gets louder.

I am going to die.

Then it hits my heart. Turns it into a glass ball. It's going to drop. Shatter. Stop. My lungs start to close in on it. It tries to escape the only way it knows how.

The dizziness comes from the heaving. The crying. The little uncontrollable whines. I sound pathetic. I will cry about this again later.

Now I'm starting to pace. At least I can pace in here. I hope that the two or three steps I can manage from one side of the broken elevator to the other- *over and over and over-* ward off the next part.

I think there's a voice coming from the speaker grate. It's warm. Fuzzy. Difficult to understand even without the panic attack.

Time flows differently when you're scared. So I'm never sure how long it takes before I start to lose my limbs.

It starts as a tingle. Malicious electricity. Then it fades. My limbs feel so numb that I don't trust them to work anymore.

3

Now I'm collapsing against the cold metal wall of the elevator cabin. I can't see where I am. I might be between floors. The door is locked. My limbs don't work. I'm alone.

You can't run out of air in an elevator. I've looked it up. Many times. But I'm not worried about running out of air. I can think of worse ways to die than asphyxiation. When you asphyxiate, you're usually lucky. You fall unconscious before you die. I'm not afraid of being unable to breathe.

It's the crushing.

It takes them thirty-two minutes to arrive. Another seven to get me out.

Thirty-nine minutes of dying.

-

I wish it stopped at panic attacks.

I was sent home from work thirty-nine minutes after arriving there. They saw the tears. Some of them heard the wails, even three floors up. I was at least spared the pitying glances that a walk to my desk would have earned me.

I trudge around my apartment all day and all evening, already in my pajamas and wrapped in a blanket. The space is so small that *trudging* is all I can do. My furniture is clunky. I have too much of it,

4

especially for the size of my apartment. Most of the pieces could barely fit through the door when I moved in. Some of them had to be disassembled and put back together again, less sturdy and with more of a creak than they had before they came here. I've tried several times to sell some of it off – listing the pieces for next to nothing, hoping to tempt some poor college kids into taking them off of my hands. But no one can be bothered to move furniture that weighs more than they do out of two doors and into a car it won't fit inside.

I only have three windows. They're distant islands to one another: gritty, double-paned rectangles that can't be cleaned properly because they have locks keeping them from opening more than four inches. It's almost not worth putting curtains on them, for the negligible amount of light they let in.

I cry again over dinner, rubbing the tears from my eyes like a child. My claustrophobia embarrasses me. It always has. I hate what it reduces me to. I hold the whimpers and moans in my throat the way you'd hold someone's head underwater. It's the only kind of mercy killing that never works.

I put off going to sleep for as long as I possibly can. But the fear has drained me – I came home exhausted, and I've spent the day struggling to keep my eyes open. I know that I'll slip into the dark as soon as I get under the covers. I'll need to get up for work again tomorrow morning. I can't put it off forever.

-

The nightmares are exactly the same. Every single time.

I'm a blink away from absolute blindness. There is nothing beyond me. *Black.* A vast, forever black that goes on farther than I could possibly fathom in every direction. I am not adrift at sea; I am adrift in space, in some blank, nowhere part of the universe after all of the stars have gone out and all of the planets have been swallowed. No one will ever find me. I am the only thing that exists in *The Eternal Nothing.*

It is not peaceful.

It is hell.

I can feel myself drifting. My thrashing and crying and screaming is in vain.

I feel it closing in on me. *The Nothing* is slowly pressing into me, at once shrinking and expanding everywhere. A paradox that will swallow me whole, just like the planets. I am going to be crushed. I am going to suffer an eternity of my own nonexistence.

I never wake up screaming or crying. I only ever wake up paralyzed.

6

I stare up at the ceiling, trying desperately to make noise. I can't. I have no control over my body.

I'm not fully awake, yet. The mattress doesn't feel solid under my back. It doesn't feel *real*. The walls warp as I feel myself sinking into it. I put everything I have into floating above it. My body is frozen, but I feel like I'm thrashing to keep myself above water.

Don't sink. Don't sink. Don't sink. Don't sink under the bed.

I know what waits under the bed. *The Nothing is there.* Just under my mattress. And if I sink, if I fall through, I'll fall into The Nothing and it will consume me.

I feel myself sinking into the blankets.

My body is heavy. *Useless.*

It starts falling through the top of the mattress.

I can't scream. I can't wiggle my fingers. I can't twitch my toes.

My eyes dart around, the equivalent of flailing, looking for something to grab onto. My room is too small. Too dark. The Nothing will come for me here, too.

My bedroom door hangs wide open. I glance into the doorway.

I glance away.

I glance back.

There's someone in the foyer.

A tall figure. A vague, hooded shape. Like a man in a cloak.

I watch it standing there.

My body sinks further.

I can't watch *and* flail.

But it's too late. I can't take my eyes off of it.

I manage a tiny whimper. *Barely there.*

The mattress stretches and thins underneath me.

Its head turns towards me.

There is something wrong under the hood.

I am gasping. I am shooting from the bed, screaming.

There is nothing in the foyer.

-

My work is quiet. The walls, floors, and furnishings of the office are all the same colour. My coworkers and my supervisors are kind, even if they don't have anything particularly interesting to say. I am paid enough to keep my tiny apartment and nothing more. My kitchen is never stocked more than sufficiently. I don't take trips and I have no one to buy gifts for. I sometimes wonder if I shouldn't have gone to school for something more interesting. But I don't know what else I would have studied.

Maybe I should have rolled a die. Maybe letting a little piece of plastic decide my future would have been better than not deciding at all.

I take the stairs instead of the elevator. I know that I look haggard today. No one says anything.

-

I still delay going to bed for as long as I can. Sometimes, if the panic attack was mild, I'll only be trapped in The Nothing for a night. But this time· wasn't mild. This time was *thirty-nine minutes* and taking the day off of work. I know The Nothing is waiting for me again.

I leave the bathroom light on when I go to bed. The light pooling past the other side of the doorway is warm enough to comfort me, but dim enough to allow me to sleep. Probably because one of the bulbs has been dead for almost a year now. The mass-produced pendant light on the ceiling is only half as alive as it should be.

-

I never get used to The Nothing. There is too much of it. When I'm awake, I wonder if it's real. I wonder if it's another dimension I slip into when I fall asleep. I wonder where my unconscious self appears in The Nothing: Do I materialize in the same spot every time? Or am I never in the same spot twice? How far do I drift? Am I really drifting? Or do I just trick myself into feeling like I am, because drifting is marginally better than being stuck?

It makes no difference. I'm still thrashing every time, wishing I could drown in an ocean instead of drowning in void. Oceans are smaller. And drowning in one would be quicker.

The irony is never lost on me – the fear of a space far too small and the fear of a space far too large coexisting like this. Manifesting one right after the other. It feels as though it should be paradoxical.

If walls threaten to crush me and space threatens to swallow me, where am I meant to feel at home?

I'm lying on my bed again, immobile, before I'm taken by the dark. I feel the sinking. The inevitable pull downwards, into the sheets and below the mattress. I resist. I struggle. It only slows the agonizing drop down.

It's there.
In the doorway.

The hooded shape reaches the very top of the doorframe. *Looming. Watching me.* I can't see Its eyes. I can barely see anything more than a dark shape. But I can feel it. *I know. It's watching me.*

Watching me sink.

Watching me stare.

And I am powerless to stop it.

Its gaze is a weight on my body. I sink faster. The bed stretches and rips like warm taffy underneath me. The Nothing is inches below me, waiting to swallow me whole.

Quiet moans of fear bleed into screams as my body wakes up, twisting in the sheets until my limbs are tangled in fabric.

-

I went to a fair on a second date once.

We sat on a bench on the boardwalk and shared ice cream & cotton candy. We looked at the water and how the lights streaked the edges of its surface. I told him that I felt like an imposter sometimes. He told me that he wanted to be a better man than his father was. We glanced away when we smiled too much, as though hiding was the polite thing to do with delight this new. We spent overpriced tickets on carnival games. He won me a plush toy bear to the soundtrack of children screaming and the music of too many attractions competing with each other. I told him that I would win him something, too.

He wanted to take me on the ferris wheel. I said, *"okay"*.

The sun had set long before. The midway was lit up beneath us. But the cabins on the ferris wheel were closed. And the lights were so, so far down.

I left the cabin hyperventilating, with tears streaming down my cheeks.

I only went on one more date with him.

I don't think he really wanted to be there.

-

I go to the drug store and buy a cheap sleep mask. I think that maybe, if I can't see anything between sleep and waking, I won't have anything to be afraid of.

I try very hard to use it. I put it over my eyes and lie back on my pillow.

I can't bring myself to keep it on.

-

The Nothing feels too big to be a simple nightmare, conjured by my own fear-ravaged brain.

It is a place I can't comprehend. It is more than apathy embodied – apathy still implies the existence of something. Absence is defined by what isn't there, but should be. Or by what *was* there, or what *will be* there. You can't have absence without the promise of existence, however brief or distant. There has never been existence in The Nothing. Just me and the dark with no beginning and no end.

I am frozen on the quicksand sheets.

It is standing at the foot of my bed.

Watching as I struggle.

I cannot resist both ways.

I cannot push myself forward *and* pull myself backward. I cannot float *and* flee.

The mattress dips and tears below me.

Down. Everything is forcing me down.

Its eyes are pushing and The Nothing is pulling. The barrier of polyester and springs falls apart. My back drops into the endless void below.

I can't claw at my bed. I can't hold myself up. My fingers refuse to respond. My whimpers are more breath than voice.

There is the shape of a jaw under Its hood. Sick confirmation that It is more than just a shape. *It has a jaw. So It must have a body. I am not imagining it when I feel It watching me.*

It is going to watch me disappear.

I am falling now. My limbs start to follow me down.

I hear someone screaming.

I'm so light-headed that I don't immediately realize it's me.

-

My mother calls me. She knows I don't go anywhere on the weekends.

The phone call lasts eighteen to twenty minutes. Every single time. Like clockwork. I ask her how she is. She mentions the pain in her stomach that she's had for months now. She keeps going to doctors' appointments. They keep telling her that the tests are coming back normal. I know that she's more worried about it than she lets on. But she won't say anything. I don't tell her about the elevator, or the panic attacks, or the nightmares. She would get uncomfortable. She wouldn't know what to say. So I don't bother.

Neither of us puts words to it. We both know that we do this.

We will probably live the rest of our lives like this. Until one of us dies. We will never know anything different.

Nothing new. Same old.

-

Nightmares can't kill you. Yet I truly believe I will die if I am consumed by The Nothing.

I've thought about anti-anxiety medication. Drugs for sleeping. But I'm scared that they'll take something from me. Make it harder to fight back. Make it impossible to keep from getting swallowed.

I don't want to find out what happens if I let it swallow me.

When I'm back on my bed, It's standing next to me.

The bed gives way underneath me.

There is the urge to stay afloat. There is the urge to shrink away, into the bed.

I have never been stalked by something like this before.

Standing as close as It is to me, I can see It emitting something. Something between substance and spectre that curls around it. *An aura. Shadow made malleable. It pulses. But far, far too slowly.*

I try to stay afloat. I can't.

The Nothing is there, under my spine. The mattress is gently releasing me into the black.

It bends over me.

There is a mouth.

I whimper through lips that refuse to move.

My hips drop. My shoulder follow. I am falling below the bed. I am half in The Nothing.

It bends closer.

There are teeth.

Too many teeth.

The Shadow twists around them. Leaks between them. Like saliva.

Like It's hungry for me.

My body is a stone. My limbs follow me down like streamers.

I am under my bed.

I can feel it from every side. The slow crushing.

It's starting.

It's coming.

I am going to die.

A hand wraps around my throat.

Palm. Fingers. Claws. Too big. They're too big.

There is no air.

I am pulled up neck-first.

I am gasping as I shoot up from the bed.

The mattress is whole. Solid underneath me. I choke on my own ragged, staccato breath.

I am awake.

I am alive.

–

I don't have any nightmares or sleep paralysis the next night. Or the next. Or the next.

I try to avoid thinking about It. But my waking hours are spent at the very edge of rumination, my mind teetering on the precipice of the spiral.

There's something about dissecting your thoughts that makes you feel more in control than you are. It's like worrying. It doesn't pragmatically help, but it *feels* like it does.

And if the problem is *feeling* like you have no control... Does worrying not, in reality, help?

The Entity pulled me out of The Nothing.

I do not believe that It wants to save me.

I do not trust that It doesn't want to hurt me.

What if It wants to kill me?

Which is better? To be at Its mercy? Or to be crushed and swallowed into eternity?

-

It is above me.

I escape The Nothing and see It. My eyes have nowhere else to go. It is here. Bent at a ninety degree angle over my body. *Over my chest.*

I try to float between two horrors.

It watches me. Unblinking. *Relentless. The Shadow* starts to seep out of it. Creeping through the air. Crawling towards me.

I feel it then. *The menace of It.* The sadistically slow stalk of a nightmare. The *it's going to get you*. The monster standing in the dark corner, waiting for your eyes to shut.

I can't do it.

I slip through the bed. The deep, silent Nothing waits to take me whole.

My body falls. But my head stays. It lolls backwards. A too-big hand wraps my neck.

It holds me by the throat. Lifts me. Raises me to Its mouth. A whimper escapes me as I am forced to look into Its jaws. Through the *too-many teeth*. Into a mouth like an abandoned well, too deep to see the bottom of. A chasm weeping a drifting, pulsing black.

I try to scream. It won't come. My heart throbs so hard that I know it will stop. It will give up any second, now. I will die of fright.

I am going to die.

I try to scream again. A small moan claws its way out of my mouth. My lips barely part- *a fraction of a fraction of an opening*. The Shadow finds the gap between them. It pours into me. It fills my mouth. Pushes into my throat. It grows. I am not merely choking. My mouth is completely and utterly filled.

I have never in my life felt this kind of *full*.

It's teeth move in slow motion above me. Jaws open just a little bit more. Shadow pools behind and between teeth. Seeps into the air between us. *Reaches for me.*

I start to feel more Shadow below me. It brushes my feet. Inches onto my skin. *Past my ankles. Up my legs.*

> *Up... up... up...*
> *Up... up... up...*
> *Over my knees...*
> *Up... up...*
> *Onto my thighs...*
> *Up... up...*
> *Up-*

The Shadow pulses harder. I cannot move. My eyes roll back as I feel it expanding deeper into my throat-

I bolt up from my pillows, gasping around the sudden absence in my mouth and the unexpected tightness between my legs.

-

The claustrophobia has always been a curse. But The Nothing is something I can forget about after a while. It's something that I can let go of. Let it fade, as dreams and nightmares always do. Distract myself and get on with my life after a few horrible nights. Even though I know it's going to come back sooner or later. In the days between the nightmares, I can live my life.

The hooded entity is more than a curse.

It haunts the edges of my mind, Its shadow always lurking in some dark crevice, just out of sight. I don't fear seeing It in the daylight- not at work, not at the grocery store, not in the street. But the thoughts are inescapable. My own head has become a vortex I can't climb out of. The intrusive memories of It looming over me, too many teeth lining a cavernous mouth, the feeling of Its darkness filling my throat and taunting my legs-

There it is again. The looking down over a high ledge *feeling, electric buoyancy between my lungs. The quick, tight ache between my legs that I can't stop myself from wanting to lean into.*

There is the fear that The Nothing gives me. A heavy, certain dread mixed with the desperation of a caged animal headed for slaughter. And then there is this.

Fear has never felt like this before.

I haven't had any more nightmares. I haven't seen It for a few days, now.

I tell myself to give it a few more days. That I'll be able to focus on my life again by the end of the week. That I'll be back to normal.

Half-way into the second week, I start taking the elevator again. Hoping it breaks down a second time.

By the end of the third week, I'm wondering where the supply closets in the office building are. I wonder if they're always locked.

PART II

I have only ever been stuck in a closet once.

When I was seven, my school did a multi-class game of Hide & Seek Tag. The doors to various rooms were left open or shut to indicate whether we were allowed to hide in them. We were all left to our own devices to either find a suitable hiding place or join the growing throng of *seekers* combing the school.

We weren't supposed to hide with friends, but many students did, anyways. I was too quiet to make friends easily, and I didn't like breaking rules, so I spent longer than I should have looking for a place to hide by myself. By the time I found the supply closet in the hallway, the designated *seekers* had already started looking for us. I don't think the closet was supposed to be left open; I think the janitors were probably just told to keep working, despite the massive game that would be going on around them. I think one of them probably left the door open a little bit by accident.

It was full of cleaning supplies. I remember because I bumped into one of the tall, wiry shelves and knocked a fat roll of scratchy brown paper towel down. I remember it hitting my foot on its way to the floor. It didn't have very much room to roll once it got there.

I remember shutting the door behind me and squeezing into a space between the wall and one of the shelves. I sat on the floor, hugging my knees to my chest, peering over a wall of plastic-wrapped toilet paper rolls.

I think about that moment now and I find myself surprised at how long I sat there... alone, but completely calm. Maybe I was distracted. Maybe I had a book or a toy with me that has faded entirely from my memory. Maybe I was so focused on watching the door and listening for footsteps that I didn't even think about where I was sitting. Time passes differently when you're a child. But I remember feeling like I was sitting there for a long time.

Eventually, either because boredom or anxiety started to kick in, I began to realize where I was. The ceiling that had felt so tall when I entered started feeling heavy. The room that had felt so spacious before – perfectly reasonable in size, I had thought – started to feel like a tomb. I began to wonder, *"what if they don't find me in here? What if nobody finds me in here? What if they forget about me?"*

When the walls started to feel like they were moving in – sneakily at first, so I wouldn't notice, all the better to trap me with – I got up and went for the door.

It didn't actually lock from the other side. I was able to turn the knob and get out.

.

I guess "stuck" wasn't the right word for it... Not stuck in the closet, anyways. Stuck with my thoughts, maybe. Stuck with my loneliness.

I can't help but think about that, now. I can't help but remember and feel like I'm returning to an old, innocent part of myself, only to offer her in sacrifice to a morbid curiosity. A temptation. A hunger.

The stakes are slightly higher when you're leaving a closet full of cleaning supplies open around small children. But when it's on the cusp of Friday evening, and you're set to spend the next few hours cleaning an empty office building, you can take a few more liberties. Or so I imagine.

I slow the pace of my walk and glance around the wide hall just behind the lobby area. My nerves start twitching under my skin, buzzing at the possibility in front of me.

It's been over a month, now.

I peer around corners. Pause my breathing to listen for the distant sounds of wheels or footsteps. My fingers curl around the strap of my bag. I step over to the door, bending down and pretending to adjust my shoe in case someone appears.

I wait. No one appears.

My stomach feels as though it's full of helium as I dip my toe into the room.

I am going to die.

Step over the threshold.

I am going to die.

Back into the closet.

One more look around. My heart flutters in warning as I disappear inside.

I am going to die.

Confined.

That's what it feels like. That's the word that keeps rolling around my head. The *confines* of this closet. *Confinement.*

I am going to die.

My hands already start to shake as I reach for the door handle. The longer I hesitate, the less I understand how my childhood self was able to stay in that closet for as long as she did. I pull my hand back. A tiny whimper escapes my throat before I take a breath and steel myself. My fingers find the handle, shaking even more than before, and my eyes begin to water. A little wave of shame comes in the form of nausea as the door floats shut.

Closets are smaller, now that I'm bigger. The lack of concern I had as a child is too far out of reach, something buried somewhere deep, in a place I haven't found yet. The latch clicks shut, muffled deep inside the thick metal frame. My fist flies to my mouth to stifle the sobs. I'm already choking around my heart. The pounding climbs up my throat. I think I'm going to cough it up. Expel it bloody and convulsing onto the old carpet. I fight to keep my hands away from the door. My feet start moving of their own accord. I immediately bump into a bucket and mop. I jump at the short clatter of plastic on plastic. I step back into a shelf. I knock over two spray bottles of cleaning fluid and some rolls of paper towel. A strangled sob comes out of me as one of the bottles starts leaking grey-blue liquid onto the floor. The closet is filled with a chemical smell. It seeps into the carpet. I could swear that the walls start moving. My eyes are closed. I'm crying. But I can feel it. *They're moving.*

My limbs start tingling. I lunge for the door.

I don't look around for witnesses. I sprint out of the building. Relief twists with embarrassment in my gut. I cry harder, praying to a God I don't believe in that nobody saw me.

-

I wanted this.

I *know* I wanted this.

Yet when I see It standing over me, taller and somehow even darker than I remember It, and Its half-shape of a half-face under a hood that looks far deeper than it should be, I still want to flee.

I'm slipping. Its stare is pushing me down into a mattress that's ripping open underneath me. I have nowhere to go. Some detached fragment of a thought falling out of the back of my head wonders if I'll ever move past the panic stage and into acceptance.

It's reaching for my neck. But I can't stop falling. Its hand is too slow.

I am going to die I am going to die I am going to die

A slow pressure closes in around my neck. My body lolls back like it's stuffed with stones. It picks me up like I'm nothing. I can feel The Shadow – on the bottoms of my feet, getting acquainted with the tips of my fingers. Shifting. Pulsing. Threatening to fill me to bursting, just like it did over a month ago.

The Shadow weaves through my fingers. Slips between them. Slips up my hands. Slips onto my feet. Claws press into my neck as a long-fingered hand pulls me closer. I am stuck looking into a sea of teeth. The Shadow rises from behind me, now. Tickles my spine. It languidly begins to consume my body from three fronts. I am powerless to stop it. I feel it deliberately crawl up my arms. My legs. Over my back and around my sides. I whimper as it reaches my thighs. Crests over my ribs. I strain to open my mouth, to make some plea to the inhuman jaws that loom over me. My body won't obey. It can't. I am as powerless to move my lips as I am any other muscle.

29

My breath starts to shake. The Shadow curls over my hips. Across my stomach. Some of it creeps upwards, under my captor's hand. Over my neck. I feel it tease the edges of my jaw. Dip into the crevices between my legs. *My groin.* I whine and try to wriggle as it makes its way towards both sets of lips, moving slowly over the soft skin. *Excruciatingly slowly.* My eyes dart in different directions, flailing in search of a life raft. They start to water. My insides tighten. Teeth begin to shift and part above me. I feel The Shadow enter me-

I can't get enough air as I jolt upright.

It takes me a few seconds to stop whining into the dark, empty bedroom.

-

I don't expect to find the supply closet open a second time.

That's alright. I'm too embarrassed to try it again, anyways. The idea of someone finding me scares me. The idea of having to explain myself – of telling the truth *or* of having to tell a convincing lie – makes my stomach roil.

I come to the conclusion that giving myself panic attacks in public is unnecessary when I have a perfectly good closet at home.

My bedroom is just as crowded as the rest of my apartment. I have to move my laundry hamper every time I want to get into my bedroom closet. It sits between the closet door and a heavy chest of drawers, which in turn imposes on the edge of my bed. I can't open the bottom two drawers without shifting my mattress over. When using the closet is unavoidable, I have to either lift the hamper onto the bed or put it on top of the chest of drawers. Getting dressed in the morning or putting away laundry becomes a puzzle game.

I slide open the doors and put my foot inside, waiting for the telltale death warning at the back of my mind. I take my time climbing in and sliding the door shut again.

It's dark and cramped inside. A faint sliver of light seeps through the bottom of the door, barely enough to see the edge of my feet by. Suddenly I can't help but think of The Entity on the other side of the door. By my bed. Waiting for me. My pulse flutters and my stomach drops.

It could be waiting for me. Staring at the closet. It could know that I'm in here.

I start to wonder if It isn't always here in my room. If It doesn't just exist here in perpetuity. Day and night. *Invisible.* Waiting for that brief window of time when I'm able to see It. I wonder if It watches me the entire time I'm sleeping. I wonder if It watches me change. I wonder if It's confined to my bedroom, or if It's able to move throughout my apartment.

There's that word again. *"Confined"*.

I wonder if It follows me outside.

My heart thumps into the cavities between my organs. The sick floating feeling of fear and the downward pull of arousal are a potent combination. I am barely clinging to reason.

But I'm still wondering why it hasn't happened, yet.

The dizziness. The crying. The *I am going to die*.

This closet is even smaller than the one I forced myself into at work. It's stuffed with clothing. There are so many hangers draped with clothes that even if I sat on the floor, I'd still have no way to avoid the hundred-layer curtain they create.

I should be crying by now. My nerves should be destroyed. I should be fighting off the overwhelming urge to escape.

Is my own closet just too familiar to trigger fear? Or have I already begun to desensitize myself?

I leave the closet. I consider reneging on my decision to avoid panic attacks in public. Shame puts me in my place again. I resolve to keep looking for confines in my own home.

I clear out the cupboard under my kitchen counter. There isn't much to clear out; I don't own any small cooking appliances, and I don't have any cookware beyond the barest essentials. My kitchen is too small to do any elaborate cooking.

I try to squeeze myself in the empty particle board box. An initial, tentative wave of fear starts to expand under my skin... but the cupboard door won't shut. I'm too big. I don't fit neatly enough for the door to seal me inside.

The cupboard in my bathroom is even smaller than the ones in my kitchen. I don't bother trying to crawl inside it.

I come back to the kitchen. My eyes land on the refrigerator. *Cold. Dark. Airtight.* I feel anxious just thinking about it.

It doesn't take long to empty and remove the shelves. I leave a milk carton standing on the floor, alongside plastic bottles with varying *best before* dates. A half-eaten pint of blueberries is gradually pushed into the baseboard of the counter and a plastic mesh onion bag leaves a trail of tiny onion-paper pieces on the tile floor. I stack the clear plastic shelves and the crisper drawers against the wall. I'm already running out of room on the kitchen floor.

My breath comes faster and heavier as I hesitantly shimmy into the refrigerator. I have to pause and shut my eyes half way in. I groan as I exhale. I sound pitiful.

The *I am going to die* is almost preferable to the *What is wrong with me?*

I scoot inside and pull the door towards me.

I have never experienced anything like the contradictory feelings of relief and disappointment I feel when the door won't shut.

I shout something gutteral and wordless as I kick the wall of the fridge from the inside.

I finish climbing out of the fridge and slouch on the floor against the cabinet doors. I wipe another stray tear from my feverish cheek. I feel like a child. *Hide and Seek and temper tantrums.* But I don't have anyone to hold me or play with me after my time-out.

I wonder if It's staring at me as I stare blankly at the floor.

I wonder if It saw the whole thing.

I can't decide which is worse: the idea that It's here watching me, or the idea that I really am all alone.

I raise my head. Brush my hair out of my face. Try to blink the sting out of my eyes. Composure is a side effect of resignation. And when it sinks in, I notice what's sitting in front of me, pressed against the wall, across from my folded body.

I can't help but think about Sylvia Plath as I take the metal grates out of my oven. I'm only a little bit older than she was when she died. Yet I haven't accomplished nearly as much as she had.

Part of me doesn't think I ever will.

As I force myself to clamber inside, I can't tell whether the tears are from fear or exhaustion.

I am going to die.

I choke as I squeeze myself into the ridged metal box.

I am going to die.

I bend to the side and pull the oven door up.

I am going to die.

The window is stained with old, yellowed grease. I almost pinch my fingers between the door and the oven.

I am going to die.

I yank it towards me, taking my hand off at the last second. It seals me in. *Quick. Final. Violently apathetic.*

Screams sound strange inside an oven.

It starts to heat up quickly. Even if it isn't turned on.

I don't remember climbing out of the oven. I only remember crying on the floor afterwards, next to a spilled carton of milk and a spray of half-crushed blueberries on the floor.

The Entity always waits until I start to sink before it reaches for me. It always watches impassively as I struggle to float. Fail. Fall.

I feel The Nothing's embrace against my back before Its hand is on me. *Around me.* Lifting my neck like the handle of a bag. *An empty bag.*

That's how I feel. *Empty.*

Desperate to be filled.

The Shadow curls and pulses over my skin. It moves over my shoulders and my neck. It pours from The Entity's hands. Escapes from between Its fingers. It moves down over my collarbones. Lower, towards my breasts. It stops just short of my peaked nipples. It changes course. *Denies me. The Shadow is cruel.* It starts moving down over my ribs. Down my back. Towards my waist.

I feel it moving up my legs. *In tandem. As above, so below.* It languidly coasts over my thighs. Around the edges of my hips.

In, towards my aching cunt.

It pulls back at the very last moment. My breath hitches in my throat. A stuttering mewl makes it out of me. The Entity watches as The Shadow expands and retracts, stroking my prickled skin.

It taunts me. It inches closer and closer to the most sensitive parts of my body... only to pull away, just *barely* out of reach.

I want to move my body. I *need* it. To shift. To twist. To angle and arch myself into The Shadow. I cannot move. My body is subject to the whim of something I can't understand.

Helpless.

Torture.

Want.

The heat builds between my legs. I feel myself grow swollen. My body cries out to be filled. I can't even moan my desire into the void.

The Shadow sways between countless teeth above me. I flail again, the way I do when I'm trying to keep myself afloat over The Nothing. I whimper. The noise is barely there. I find myself begging. Pleading in thought. Grovelling in silence.

I don't know if It can even *hear* my thoughts.

Please. Please. Do something with me. Do anything. Please. Anything you want. Please-

The Entity's free hand slowly appears and lifts from Its side. It moves towards my body. *Torturously slow.* It hovers over me. Scans my body until it reaches my chest.

I watch, insufferably still. I can't even tremble as it lowers one massive, inhumanly long, clawed finger to my skin. It traces Its claw over my collarbone. Over my breast. It makes agonizing, deliberate circles around my nipple. I whimper, wishing to squirm away. The touch that teases the

37

very tip of my breast is too light. It drags Its claw across my chest. Repeats Its circles on my other nipple. They are just as unbearable as they were the first time.

Ages pass. It raises Its hand again. With one hand still on my neck, the other coasts down my body. *So close to touching my skin.*

It until it lands on my leg. Slips down to my inner thigh. Drags into the precious little space between one leg and another. *Dangerously close to my cunt.*

It pushes Its palm against my leg. It moves my limb likes it weighs nothing. My second leg mirrors the first, drifting open. I am swiftly spread wide apart. I am unable to crane my neck or look down. I swear that I can feel the cool touch of The Shadow brush against my folds. Every immodest, hidden inch of me is exposed to The Entity.

It raises Its hand again. Replaces Its finger in the hollow at the base of my neck. Drags Its claw in a slow, slow line down my chest.

Please...
Between my breasts.
Shadow dripping like appetite from Its teeth...
Down my stomach.
Oh, God...
Over my mound.
Claws...

Towards my cunt.

It's going to rip me apart from the inside.

Renewed terror consumes me.

It lifts Its hand. Twists it. Angles two fingers towards my opening. I watch the vicious claws sink lower. Lower. I try to scream. I can't. I feel It. Inhuman fingers press slick folds-

It slips inside me.

My failed screams melt into muffled moans.

I don't feel claws. There is no pinch. No *sharp*. Only fingers. *Long fingers. Pushing inside me.* I feel them curve into me. Pressing into the soft flesh deep inside me. *Under my clit.* They slide in and out of me. *Slow. Excruciating.* I hear my own wetness in the spaces between uneven breaths.

I feel myself expand. My eyes dart down. Three long digits thrust in and out of me. Massage every inch of my cunt from the inside.

I strain to move my hips in time with Its thrusts. I can't.

I think that It must keep me this way. *Paralyzed.*

It's been so long. *So, so long.* Every cell in my body begs for release.

It slips a fourth finger into me. Another moan crashes against my teeth. Throws itself at my lips.

It's still too slow. I can think of nothing beyond this. *Senseless need. Desperation. I need to come.*

The Entity denies me this mercy. It keeps me a hair's breadth from the edge. Traps me there. *Confines me. Climax just out of reach.*

Please please please I'm begging you please oh my God please-

My cunt is soaking wet. It curves Its hand lengthwise. *Fingers extended. Pressed into one another.* It and pushes inside me.

I open wider. I sob in pleasure. The sound is too small. Half of Its hand enters me. It is deep. *So, so deep.*

Slow thrusts.

In and out.

In and out.

In and out.

Fucking me until my eyes water.

It takes Its time. *There is no time here. It has eternity.*

It fucks me faster. The pace steadies. Grows.

More...

Faster...

More...

More...

MORE...

I can't hold on. I'm thrown over the edge-

I am trembling as I wake. I feel only the very last pulses of my orgasm; it's as though I blacked out for the few, explosive seconds of bliss that I had so desperately craved.

When I eventually move and pull back the sheets, I find a splotch of blood underneath my hips.

I head to the bathroom to clean up the first stains of my period before I strip the sheets.

-

I start to doubt myself when I try to climb back into the oven and find that I can't fit inside.

It's easy to write off a sudden need to test the limits of your deepest fears. *Humans are inherently self-destructive*, I could tell myself. Everyone engages in some form of self-destruction. Their own niche flavour of emotional masochism. Maybe after feeling nothing for so long, my brain has gotten hooked on the experience of feeling something. Feeling *anything*. Any rush is a temptation to chase. Even a rush of fear.

I used to be fine feeling nothing. I used to be content. When you lock yourself into complacency, it's easy to believe that all of the other emotions banging on the other side of the door will eventually go away.

41

But my hinges broke. I got stuck in that elevator. Thrown back into The Nothing and spat out, only to find something inhuman lurking on the other side of the door.

I think I prefer to believe that The Entity is real, in some sense. Because it's easier to blame something I can't understand than it is to be confronted with the possibility of not being able to trust my own mind.

Questioning my sanity because I want to climb into an oven is logical. I can still come to the conclusion that I'm perfectly sane, simply *because* I'm asking myself whether or not I'm sane. But questioning my sanity because I don't fit inside an oven that I fit very neatly into the other day doesn't give me the same kind of reassurance.

There is an enormous difference between not being able to trust your motivations and not being able to trust your memory.

I don't know what's worse: The impaired perception of reality, or the fact that I keep trying to find ways to confine myself, anyways.

I spend an hour considering every inch of my cluttered apartment. I shuffle along the walls and sidestep between family-sized furniture looking for hidden crevices that I can squeeze myself into. No drawer or cabinet is big enough to hold me. Neither the legs of the couch nor the heavy armchair that's crammed next to it are high enough off of the floor that I'm able to crawl underneath.

I end up in my bedroom again and briefly lie on the floor, next to my bed. There's barely enough room for my back to lay flat. I'm tightly sandwiched between the long edge of the bed and the wall. I turn my face to the side and peer underneath the bed. My heart skips a beat, half-expecting to find The Entity looking back at me. But there's nothing.

I think about shimmying sideways. I think that I might just barely fit underneath the bedframe, lying flat on my back like this.

I can't stop thinking about The Nothing waiting for me under there.

I get up from the floor so quickly that I make myself light-headed.

I can't do it.

-

I don't have my own in-unit washing or drying machine. If I want to do laundry, I have to go all the way down to the basement.

The laundry room is small. It's filled with half a dozen washers and dryers each, all pay-per-load. There are a couple of plastic chairs against the wall by the door.

I try going down during the day. I sit in one of the chairs, feeling self-conscious that I didn't even bring some laundry with me. I can't help feeling like people will see through me, somehow. They'll know that I'm not actually waiting for my clothes or my sheets to finish their cycle. They'll know that none of the swirling maelstroms of fabric are actually mine. I shrink into the chair every single time someone walks through the door. I'm convinced that they'll take one look at me and know why I'm really here.

I wait for almost an hour before I get up and leave. There are too many people using the machines right now. I should have thought of that.

I stay up late and walk back down at two-thirty AM. I intentionally keep myself awake until then, reasoning that my exhaustion will help facilitate a panic attack.

Every machine sits empty, except for one washing machine rattling away, cycling a mass of soapy clothes inside. The ball in my stomach rises and drops as I check the timer, weighing how long I have before the owner of the clothes comes to move them to the drying machine.

I don't remember how long I was in the oven for. What if I lose track of time again? What if I'm found hyperventilating and crying on the floor? Or worse-

I stop thinking about it and just move. I can't stand it anymore. I'm pushed forward by a hot, urgent need to just get it over and done with already.

I open the door to one of the side-loading washing machines and ball myself up inside.

The windowed door curves in towards me, pressing into my thigh and my upper arm as it closes. The metal barrel shifts underneath me as I squirm, refusing to settle. *I am going to die* is punctuated by the feeling of countless little drainage holes against my skin. There's no one on the other side of the machine door, no coins or cards to spur the machine on, but I still imagine it filling with water.

I am going to die.

The barrel continues to rock with my heartbeat. I begin to rock my body response. My feet start to feel wet. I squeeze my knees into my chest. I wail into them. When my face comes away, there are already wet spots where my eyes were. Water is pooling at the bottom of the barrel.

There is no pacing in here. No space for anxious fidgeting. Just the belly of an old, metal appliance. Rocking me deeper into fear. Into a blackout. Like a mother rocks a crying baby.

Little streams of water streak down my back. Under my shirt. My toes are submerged.

The next thing I remember, I'm lying on the cold tile floor of the laundry room. My clothes and

45

my skin feel damp. I'm shivering. All of the appliances are empty. The room is silent, save for the inescapable background hum of ventilation.

Whomever came to dry and collect their clothes must not have seen me. Or did see me, and didn't bother to say or do anything.

I don't know which one makes me feel worse.

-

Something is different the next night.

I don't dream after I get back from the laundry room. I barely sleep at all. I call in sick to work the next day and spend it waiting instead. I don't know what I'm waiting for. Somehow I know I won't see It during the day. I still try to avoid napping on my couch anyways, just to be safe.

I fail. But I try.

When I see The Entity waiting for me after I fall asleep the next night, It's standing at the foot of my bed.

I've come to expect Its face to be nearer. Looming over me with Its jagged maw and Its threatening hands. But It just stands there. Staring.

The mattress begins its slow decay. It starts to rip open under me. I flail with a renewed desperation.

What if It knows? What if It knows what I've been putting myself through, just to submit myself to Its terrors again and again?

I'm certain.

In that moment, between the monster and the void, I'm sure that It knows.

I have been doing this to myself. I have wanted this. I'm sick. I'm *vile*. I'm so irredeemably deranged that I don't just *want* to taken and possessed by this creature. I *thirst* for it.

This is my punishment. The very ruin I would turn myself inside out for, watching apathetically as I fall into eternal Nothing.

I can't even tell myself that I don't deserve it.

I feel the pull of empty space below me. My body continues to sink, caving into The Nothing.

The Entity drops.

Not *bends over*. Not *sinks to Its knees*. It *drops*. Below the edge of the mattress.

I take it back.

This is my punishment.

Abandonment.

The sting of tears rims my eyes. I flail.

A dark shape reappears at the edge of the mattress. Past my feet.

A massive hand crests the bed. Then another. Claws dig into sheets. The Entity pulls Itself over. It slowly crawls over the bed.

The bed expands as It crawls towards me. Stretches. *Lengthens.* Its shoulders move up and down. It prowls towards me. Stalks me. My heart stutters. I can do nothing.

It's going to get me.

Its stare is palpable. Menacing. Hungry.

It's going to get me.

Primal fear. Sprinting up the stairs in the dark. Terrified of what's at the bottom.

It's going to get me.

It's going to get me.

My shoulders sink. My back. I fall backwards. Down. Past the mattress. Towards The Nothing.

I see Nothing.

Clawed hands reach my thighs. My legs part. I am pried open. Legs thrown to either side. I am powerless to resist.

My hips follow the rest of me. They sink.

Hands.

Claws.

They're on my hips. *Colossal. Pulling.*

I feel tiny. Helpless. Its fingers curve around my hips. Dig into my flesh. The Shadow leaks from them. Trails over my skin. Leaves goosebumps in its wake. It curls over my thighs. Dips into the creases of my groin. It pulses over the thin, sensitive skin around my cunt. Shows me how wide I've been spread. How exposed I am to the endless-deep hood and those deep-sea teeth.

My breath is shallow. I wait. I can do nothing else. I'm whimpering. Pathetic. Begging once again.

Please, please, do anything to me...

Please...

Take me.

The Shadow pulses. Gathers between my legs. Presses at my entrance.

I feel it. The brush of teeth on my lips. I wince. My eyes dart between my breasts. Over my stomach. I watch The Entity's hood rise over my cunt.

Its jaw opens. A long, dark tongue slips from between Its teeth. *Too long.*

The Entity lowers Its head.

I feel Its gaze on me like a restraint.

Its tongue finds my aching, wet cunt.

My whimpers become moans. It explores me. Claims every inch of my cunt as Its own. *Flesh conquered.* It laps between my lips. Over my clit. It plunges into me. Back out again. Swirls my own arousal onto my clit.

My body screams. Needs to move. Needs to rock my hips into Its tongue. Craves the certain destruction of Its teeth.

My pleasure builds. I am certain that It could rip me to pieces. *Like nothing.* Swallow me whole. Without a second thought.

49

I inch closer to release.

I no longer care.

The Entity tortures me. Keeps me teetering on the brink. It pushes me to the edge. Pulls me back. Brings me to the edge again. Pulls me away. *Pushes. Pulls. Pushes. Pulls.* I continue to moan through a mouth that's sealed shut. I sob into the pleasure. Into my helplessness to stop it. My helplessness to hasten it.

Its tongue pleasures me faster. Harder.

I can't hold on anymore. Everything falls away. I surrender to my climax, my cunt clenching-

I wake up moaning and soaking wet. My fingers find their way between my legs. They plunge into my cunt.

I can't let this go.

More.

I need more.

PART III

The salesman at the used car dealership doesn't know that I don't have a driver's license.

I went online and looked for the most poorly-reviewed used car dealership in the city. I thought that going somewhere less professional — ideally somewhere with more questionable business practices — would make what I'm planning to do easier. But I can't deny that I also thought I might have an easier time doing it if the staff were rude to me.

I don't know why I thought that spite would embolden me. It never has been before.

The salesman is only a little bit condescending to me. He has brown hair and glasses. He says his name at one point, but I'm too nervous to remember it.

I had braced myself to look at a few different cars before I enacted my plan. I want to look convincing. I want it to look as though I was genuinely shopping around. But my nerves are frayed. I'm certain that the longer I stayed here talking to him, pretending that I'm actually interested in buying a car, the closer I am to being found out.

When I see a car at the far edge of the lot, parked parallel to the building, in a blind spot to most of the windows, I awkwardly ask to look at it.

I try to listen to what he tells me about the vehicle. But it won't stick. I can't retain what make or model it is. I'm too nervous. It doesn't matter, anyways. The only thing I notice is that it's red.

I ask to see inside the trunk. *I need to see how big it is,* I tell him. *I'm an artist. I want to see if it's big enough to carry my equipment.* He asks me what kind of art I do. I tell him I paint.

It makes me sad to tell him that. I don't think I ever could have been a painter. Even if I wanted to.

He says something about his brother-in-law painting. Or maybe someone else's brother-in-law. I nod my head. Pretend I'm hearing him. He goes to get the key. My hands won't stay still. I put them on the car. I hold them in front of me. Hold them behind my back. Put them in my pockets. I do anything I can think of to stop them from shaking.

He comes back. He pops the trunk open for me. I look inside the trunk, pretending I'm assessing it for something reasonable. Something normal. He's too close to me. I have to make something up on the spot to get him to move. I ask him if this was the one with the scratch on the front. He furrows his brow and says he doesn't think so. He walks around to the front to take a look and I sneak the tiny wood wedge out of my pocket. I slip it between the door of the trunk and the body of the car. As he's bent over, inspecting the paint, I close the trunk. It shuts without latching, just enough to look like it's really closed. He walks back around. Confirms that there's no scratch.

I put my hands on my bag, squeezing the strap to keep the trembling at bay. He asks if I want to take the car for a test drive. Jingles the keys in front of me like a canapé at a Christmas party. I decline and ask to look at another car.

A thrill pierces my stomach – he didn't notice me putting the wedge in. My plan is working. I get the distinct feeling that I've inherited a power that isn't really mine: The power to make people second-guess themselves.

After we take a look at another car- a white sedan that's seen better days- I feign dissatisfaction and make excuses to leave. He tries to sell me on another vehicle, but I panic and say I need time to think about the options.

I wander away, looking over my shoulder the whole time. Once he's back inside and out of sight, I head to towards the side of the lot, where the red car sits by the edge of the building. My heart pounds as I slip behind it.

Pry open the trunk.

I am going to die

Fear pushes me inside with a whimper. I curl myself into a ball and bite my fist – *I am going to die* – as I tumble into the trunk and pull the door shut behind me.

Cl-click.

The little wedge of wood I brought with me lies by my feet. I was too quick climbing inside. In my haste, I knocked it aside. Kicked it towards the opposite end of the trunk.

Now it's locked in here with me.

I am going to die.

My heart is rioting. I'm certain it's making the entire car shake. I wail into the floor of the trunk. Tears stream down my hot face. I bang on the door. On the sides of the trunk. On the back of the seat. My fists pound everywhere within reach.

This car is going to start shrinking on me. I'm sure of it. I didn't buy it. *I rejected it.* And now they don't need it anymore, because they didn't sell it to me. Now they're going to take it to get impounded and I'm going to be stuck inside the whole time. I'm going to be crushed to nothing inside this car, and they aren't even going to watch it happen, they're just going to put it under the machine and turn their backs and walk away while I get crushed and no one will ever know what happened to me and I'll be lost forever –

And who would care?

The thought is invasive. Cruel. *Sound.*

What would it matter if I disappeared? Who would miss me?

Who would notice?

I just cry harder.

I'm getting light-headed. The dizziness sets in. The car shifts around me.

I hear a *clunk*. Feel the distant slamming of a door. *The driver's door.* Embarrassment gives in to desperation. I scream again. The engine starts. I keep screaming. *Help. Please. Help.* I bang on the back of the seat. The driver doesn't hear me. The car starts to move.

I'm so dizzy. I don't know where we're going.
The tail lights. Kick out the tail lights.

I twist my body around. Face the back of the car. It's pitch black. I can't see. I feel around for the tail lights. I try to figure out where to kick –

...*No.*

There's something wrong.

I can't find them.

I twist and turn. Run my hands over every inch of the trunk. It doesn't matter. They're not there.

There are no tail lights. Just metal and carpet. A capsule with no exit.

The engine revs. The car speeds up. I'm jerked and shaken around with every bump. Every pothole.

I've never googled whether you can run out of oxygen in a car trunk or not.

I keep beating the car. I sob. The car keeps moving. My limbs begin to buzz. They go numb.

The trunk begins to shrink. I know it does. It compresses with every breath. Every single exhale. One more inch of space gone. It shouldn't be possible. But it's happening. I feel it.

Smaller.

Smaller.

Smaller.

I'm hyperventilating.

Smallersmallersmallersmallersmallersmaller —

My legs are useless. I pull them in. Squeeze them to my body. Try to make myself as small as I can.

It won't be long.

I am going to die in this speeding car —

-

I don't remember falling unconscious any more than I remember waking up.

When I come back to myself, I'm already walking. I think I have been for a while.

I'm trudging up a street in a neighbourhood I don't recognize. It's vaguely industrial. A couple of nondescript, blocky concrete buildings are scattered around the wide stretch of road. It's after dark. There's no one else around. The streetlights are all out, except for one ahead of me. It's little more than a fuzzy dot of light in the distance.

When I reach it, I stand underneath it and look down at my clothes. They're covered in dirt. I'm covered in scuff marks. I have no idea where they came from. My hair is a tangled mess. There's a rip in the shoulder of my shirt.

I look out into the dark from my little island of light. The night is quiet. There are no crickets. No faraway *zooms* of cars on the highway. There's a slight chill, but no breeze to speak of. I look up. There are no stars. Just a dark, muted sky over a dark, muted world.

The longer I stand there, the more the pool of light seems to shrink. It doesn't flicker or wink above me. It just dims, the circle around me slowly edging closer and closer to my feet.

Another streetlight glows up ahead, another distant speck of ghostly yellow.

I walk towards it. Step under it. Listlessly gaze into the dark as it starts to dim.

My eyes eventually glaze over. I stop thinking as I follow the beacons home.

I don't know how long I walk for.

Time passes differently when there's no *scared* left in you.

I forgot to call in sick to work.

I guess it doesn't really matter. I've used up all of my sick days by now.

My phone rings twice. I know it's them, even without seeing the company's name on the caller ID. Who else would call me?

I let it ring both times.

-

I still fight The Nothing. I still strain. Struggle as though The Entity might not show up this time.

When I open my eyes, It's not at the foot of my bed.

It's right above me. On my ceiling.

Its back is pressed to the popcorn ceiling. As though It would float away without it. *Sword of Damocles. Helium and teeth.*

My bed begins to tear. It starts to float down. *Slowly.*

I struggle. But I am learning to trust It.

It places Its hand over my stomach. My body drapes under It. *Limp. Useless.* Head and feet dangle languidly above the abyss.

I have to peer over my nose and past my chin to see into the endless hood. Its jaw moves. Teeth appear. Pale peaks multiply as Its lips- *are there lips?*- peel back. They create a gash in the shadow of the hood.

Its tongue slips from between Its teeth. It is too long. The Shadow twist around it like ivy. It grows longer... longer... longer... It tastes my jaw. I repress a shiver that won't come. I whimper in protest and pleasure. It traces the line of my jaw. Down my neck. Onto my chest.

I need more.

I need more than to be sampled.

I need to be devoured.

It glides Its tongue over my nipple. My breath skips in my throat. Nerves lighting up like fireworks under my flesh. The muscles between my legs clench. It twists Its tongue around my nipple and squeezes. Pulls. Claims. *How do I taste?* I want to ask. *Do I please you?*

Is it good?

Is it enough to make you stay?

Teasing turns into delicious pain. It squeezes harder. Its tongue moves down. Slowly coasts over my stomach. The Shadow creeps up my body to cup my breasts. Hold my thighs.

The Shadow continues to torment my nipples. The monstrous tongue edges my mound. My groin. The cleft where my lips meet.

My legs drift apart, The Shadow guides them open as The Entity sinks between them. It hovers between my legs. Its hips are level with mine, It pulls Its tongue back behind the endless mountains of hacksaw teeth.

I feel my own wetness dripping out of me. My cunt aches. I am an empty vessel. Waiting to be filled.

The Shadow crawls over my body. Towards my glistening lips. Spreads them open. Teases my entrance.

The Entity seems even larger. *Even more inescapable.*

I understand it now. What we are to each other. We are *hungry* for one another.

I feel something pressing into me. *Pushing* into me. Slowly entering me –

I blink awake with a needy moan. I cover my ears. I've been awoken by something loud. Relentless.

I growl.
The fire alarm.
Interrupted.
Ripped away.

I won't get up. I can't leave it there. I need to be sated. I need release.

62

The alarm conceals my moans as I put my hand between my legs. I've started sleeping naked. I plunge my fingers into my cunt, soaking them with my arousal. I rock my hand over my entrance. Press the heel of my palm *just so* over my clit. I moan aloud, heedless of neighbours. I feel myself inch closer to the edge.

It's not enough. I need *It*.

I climb on top of my covers. Lie back. Spread my legs wide. I lay my head back on the pillow and relax my body into stillness. I try to mimic my own paralysis as pleasure myself.

I shut my eyes. I imagine It filling me. *Taking me* —

I cry out as the climax crashes over me. Pleasure rushes through muscles that tense and release into its waves.

Take me, I think as I come, wondering if It can hear me. *Take me*.

-

I've been forgetting to go into work at all.

It's easy to lose track of what day of the week it is when you forget to go into work.

There are several voicemails on my phone. They're all from the office. I play them on speakerphone. I only half-listen. I'm distracted, scrolling through the first page of results on the search engine.

I'm pretty sure they just said something about letting me go.

That's okay. I can listen to it again later.

I return to the list of funeral homes within bussing distance.

-

Apparently, it's very common to consult with a funeral director and view the home's selection of urns & caskets before a loved one's death has actually occurred.

I tell them that my father is in the hospital. I tell them that he's near the end and I want to explore my options.

People handle grief in different ways. I have to worry less about being convincing. It makes this meeting easier than the one at the car dealership.

I've never been in a casket showing room before. I hadn't taken the time to research what to expect, either. My desperation made me naïve. Now I've run into a problem at the funeral home.

I was expecting a room lined with caskets that you could open and examine as you wished. What I'm shown instead is a room with six full caskets, each with their lids propped open to display their interiors, and a catalogue wall of casket corner sections.

The funeral director is patient as they show me the options. I nod and respond in bland affirmatives to the gentle explanations that come from their mouth.

A closet door is meant to be be shut. A car's trunk is meant to stay closed. But these caskets are here to be peered into. There's no hiding inside them.

I ask if they have any other caskets available to see. They tell me they don't, and that I can consult the catalogue wall for more options.

They leave me alone for a few minutes to consider the displays.

I *could* slip inside one of these caskets. I could do it right now. While the funeral director is gone. I could shut the lid and hope that I leave reality again. Inexplicably come back somewhere strange, just as I did after the car. But I can't risk that. Not in the daylight. The casket isn't a mobile vessel. It's not an enclosure that lives outside. It's a heavy box that's stuck in a room with fading carpet and a window that doesn't open.

There may be an escape from the box, but there won't be an escape from discovery.

I check the time. Over five hours until the funeral home closes. Who knows how much longer until everyone is gone.

I sigh. Run my hands over my face. Grit my teeth.

I will do it.

I walk carefully out of the room. Keeping an eye out for the funeral director, I wander – *innocently wander* – the halls of the funeral home. I pull at door handles. Peek into rooms. I turn a corner. My breath catches. I see the funeral director, their back to me, on the cusp of turning. I duck back behind the wall. Creep down a short, adjacent hall. Turn the knob on the door at the end. I expect a room or closet to slip into. It opens. I almost stumble down the set of stairs on the other side. I silence my gasp with my fist.

Around the corner, the funeral director emerges from the other side of the wall. I tiptoe down the stairs and shut the door, quickly and softly. *Before they see. Before I can rethink what I'm doing.*

I haunt the dim halls of the basement. My feet pad gently over the linoleum. Muted metal sounds from down the hallway tell me that I'm not alone here.

There's a wide metal door coming up on my left. The sounds are coming from behind it. I sneak closer. My heart thumps louder than my footfalls. I creep close enough to touch the door. Brush my fingertips over it. Press my ear to the cold metal. The sound isn't the sound of a machine. It isn't a furnace or a water heater. There's a person in there. *Doing something*. Going about their work.

I can't bring myself to keep listening. The thought of getting caught here, before I can find what I need, makes me want to jump out of my skin.

I move away from the door. Dip around a corner on my right. There's another door. I don't hear any sound behind it.

It's unlocked.

I twist the handle and delicately push it open.

The casket storage room is much bigger than the showroom. Various caskets lie stacked together, shelved next to and on top of each other.

I can't help but think about all of the empty shoe boxes my grandparents kept in the closet, tucked away to use as gift boxes for Christmases and birthdays. They kept so many of them that most of them didn't get used. Dozens of boxes lay stacked behind a slatted folding door in the basement, collecting dust.

I played with them a handful of times as a child. Sorted them and used them as building blocks, carefully crafting my own castles and walls.

I found a dead mouse in one of them, once.

It scared me, to imagine it dying in that dark little cardboard box.

I screamed, and I'm sure one of my grandparents cleaned it up. Likely threw away the box.

But I thought about that mouse over the next few years. Wondered just how *forgotten* it was. Had my grandparents forgotten about it too, as soon as they threw it in the trash? Had the mouse's parents forgotten it? Its littermates? Its children? Was I the only person in the whole world who remembered it?

Sometimes I still scare myself. Thinking about how, when I'm gone, that mouse's tiny, insignificant life will have never existed.

I think memory is the only thing that tethers you to the world. And that forgetting is the only thing that can reach all the way back into the past and change reality. If everyone you've ever seen or touched forgets about you, then you no longer exist anymore. You never did.

I think that's why The Nothing scares me. Because I know that I'm very forgettable.

I run my fingers over the edge of the casket lids. Trace their smooth, lacquered edges.

Forgetting boxes. That's all they are.

The sound of footsteps in the hall set my nerves on fire. I swallow the tears beginning to line my eyes. The lump that's starting to choke me. I lift the lid of the casket in front of me. I climb inside as quickly as I can and shut myself in.

I try to stifle my breathing as the footsteps near the door. Reach it. Walk past it.

My veins quiver under my skin while I wait for inevitable discovery. My stomach churns and coils. My skull feels lighter than air.

The footsteps return. The door to the room opens. I hear the *step... step... step* of a body circling the room. Shoes are flattened by old, worn-flat carpet. Tears tease needles under my eyes. A whimper threatens the back of my throat.

The soft *plunk* of a hand finds the wood above me.

Every second their hand lingers on the casket lid stretches my willpower. All it will take is a few inches. *Unseen fingers, finding the ledge. Lifting the lid.* All it will take is a few seconds. I'll be found out.

This casket was open when I got here. It's *supposed* to be open.

I am trapped. I have made myself prey to happenstance.

Fingertips slide across the wood, just above my face. They slip off of the lid. Disappear beyond perception. A moment later, there is a soft, distant *click*.

The room – and soon, the hallway – are both quiet again.

I take a trembling breath. I wait for it. The *I'm going to die.* The rebellion in my chest. My body trying to claw its way out of itself.

It takes longer than I expect.

I shut my eyes. My hands find their way to my sides. I feel the tight, hard edges of the casket. I feel the lid. *The heavy, satin-lined lid.* It promises to suffocate me. To sink lower and lower until it crushes me. *Destroys me. Stains the inside of the box with my last breaths and every last drop of every last fluid in my body.*

-

I've briefly forgotten where I am.

I open my eyes and find that it makes no difference. I'm blind here.

Black.

My hand finds the inside of the casket again. It doesn't even startle me. I've fallen asleep and woken back up, with no clue what time it is.

The worst part is that It hasn't come for me. The Entity hasn't found me.

Tears burn the edges of my eyes. *I have failed It*, I can't stop myself from thinking. *It doesn't want me. My fear wasn't good enough. I'm insufficient. I wasn't able to summon a suitable offering.*

I feel like a child, wiping the heel of my hand over my cheeks. *Please. I can do better, please.*

It is a quiet and slow climb out of the casket. The room is unforgiving – there are no windows, nor a slice of light under the door to offer any light. There is nothing to guide my hesitant, clumsy steps.

I try to trick myself into thinking that The Entity might be here with me, standing in the dark where I can't see It. I search for the addictive, *dropping* feeling in my stomach. Dig for it. *Get dirt under my nails.* The fear. The arousal. The anticipation of a forced surrender. *I am my own graverobber.*

I'm still trying to unearth it as I slowly open the door and step into the dark hallway.

I feel along the walls. I check doors. My hands find the metal door I passed earlier. I press my ear to the edge of it: *Silence.*

The handle gives way with a whining *click* as I press the weight of my hand onto it. The door opens with a soft moan. I step into the tiled room.

It smells chemical in here. *Antiseptic.* There are drains in the floor and an empty, wheeled table near the middle. Cabinets line one edge of the room. A large metal sink is flanked by massive plastic jugs.

I jump when the vent at the top of a nearby wall starts up. It briefly rumbles to life before quieting again.

I've never felt like the most alive thing in a room, before. I've never been somewhere like *this*, before. It is clinically quiet. A liminal space between life and death. This is where bodies are baptized in chemicals before being closed up in their *forgetting boxes*, pretty and pristine and ready to be swallowed by The Nothing hiding under the dirt.

There is a massive steel structure against the right-hand wall.

There is something unreal about it. It emanates the *feeling* of silence. Of stillness. Of finality. It is too eerie to be holy. It is too sacred to be ignored.

I find myself walking over to the polished metal giant without thinking. It is as though my body already knows where to go.

The sound of my footsteps remind me that I am a trespasser here. My fingers trace the doors of the refrigeration unit. Fear moves through me like a slow thunder. I wonder if there are any bodies inside. I wonder how many. I wonder what would happen if I joined them. Would the mortician find me in the morning, just as dead as everything else inside? Would they embalm me? Hold a funeral for me – like parents hosting a birthday party for their child – only for none of their classmates to show up? Would the staff remember me? The lonely woman who crept into a funeral home, like a cat curling up under a porch just to die? *Would they remember me? Would that keep The Nothing away for a little while longer?*

No. I know what keeps The Nothing away.

My heart sputters as fear roils in my stomach. I feel my groin grow slick, from sweat or arousal. I feel myself clench as a whimper escapes my throat.

I can do better. Please, I can do better for you.

72

I strip.

My body moves between excitement and reverence, taking each item of clothing off one by one and dropping them to the chilled tile floor.

I stand there, completely naked, pressing my fingers to the sterile-cold door.

I open it with a trembling hand.

I crawl into the middle rack. I wince at the feeling of cold metal on my bare skin.

So, so cold.

I let the door swing shut at my feet.

I think there's a body above me.

I can't tell in the dark.

I lie back on the shelf, my body completely stretched out. I let the cold taste every inch of my skin. It is both sacrament and punishment. My flesh prickles and my nipples harden into peaks. I can't see the mist of my breath in this liminal crypt.

I shut my eyes and silently call for It. *Beg for It.*

Please.

I am here.

I am laid out for you. Your sacrificial virgin. Untouched. Do with me as you please.

Make me something.

I feel the ball-drop sensation in my stomach as my body arches backwards. It is the helpless jolt one feels before a freefall. A split-second of terror overtakes me before I feel It.

You save me.

I am laid bare for you. I surrender myself to you. How may I thank you?

As The Shadow slowly finds my skin, I feel Its hand- *so much bigger, now*- trace claws down my collar, my breasts, my stomach, my mound...

My hips rise, as though pulled by a string.

Yes. I am your puppet. Play with me. Control me.

It holds me aloft by my cunt, exposing every last naked inch between my legs as the rest of my body dangles below It. I feel It looking. *Examining me.* I try to squirm. I can't. Breathy whimpers turn into mewling moans as The Shadow crawls over my skin, kissing chills onto my nipples. My hips. My neck.

My head falls back, baring my neck to The Entity. It's so much bigger, now. *Colossal. Monstrous.* I feel as though It could open Its jaws and swallow me whole. *A tender, juicy morsel begging to be consumed.* Its massive hand finds its way to my throat. Long, heavy fingers and claws several inches long encircle my neck. Press into my jaw. Hold me in place while The Shadow slips towards my mouth and between my legs. It takes its time spreading me wide, top and bottom. It bares both of my wet, hungry caverns to the void.

How well I have learned to surrender.

My mouth and my cunt clench as something starts to enter them both in tandem. It slips bit by agonizing bit between my soft, parted entrances. Lingers, just barely inside me. I feel Its firmness, Its soft pulse as It pushes further.

I'm so wet. *So tight.*

It pushes deeper inside me, slowly stretching me open in both holes. I feel as though I could choke. I feel fuller than I've ever felt in my entire life. Physically. Emotionally. *Spiritually.* I have never been so *filled.*

I am your vessel.
Fill me.
Fill me.

The Entity buries itself deep inside me. When I don't think that It can go any deeper, it keeps pushing. It *keeps* filling me.

Let me be full of nothing but You.

The pulsing grows stronger in my mouth and my cunt. It begins thrusting.

In. Out. In. Out.

It brings me to the edge of euphoria and keeps me there. *Refuses to let me climax.* Keeps me in a state of indefinite *almost,* perpetual pre-bliss.

The rhythm is constant. It never stops. It just keeps pulsing, keeps thrusting until my mind goes blank with suspended pleasure. There are no thoughts. There are no troubles. There is no loneliness. Only this perfect trance of euphoria.

Yes. Trance.

The orgasms come over me at regular intervals. They pass through my body, leaving waves of peace every single time.

Trance.
Come.
Peace.
Trance.
Come.
Peace.

-

I return to my work building to collect my things. I'm surprised that they held onto my belongings for as long as they did.

Not that I had much at my desk, anyways.

My belongings won't even fill the box I'll be taking them home in.

I'm not worried. I'm not scared. I can find another job. It doesn't even have to be a good one. Or a full-time one. I don't need much. A little food. A roof over my head. That's really it.

I bet I can find something remote. That way, I won't need too many clothes. I won't need my cell phone, either. I can cancel my plan. I can get rid of all

76

of my furniture and move somewhere smaller. *Yes... much, much smaller. That would be perfect.* I can forego having a bed entirely. I don't need one. I can sleep in something small. *Something tight.* A long console cabinet. A large aquarium or terrarium. A hot water tank with an opening cut just large enough to wiggle through.

I have nothing to be afraid of. Fear has become holy.

I step into the elevator.

This elevator.

It feels so right, that my new life should start where my old one ended. This is my hallowed ground. My *forgetting box.* My ascension to the Sacred Void.

The elevator rises. I prepare to collect my trivial belongings from this place, see everyone here for the last time.

They don't know.

They don't know that I have found something greater.

The elevator stutters and stops between floors.

Again, I think. *Again...*

The lights inside the cabin flicker. Buzz. Go out.

I bask in the shuddering breath that ripples through me like the start of an earthquake. Sweet terror flutters in my gut. It rises up, an electric blade under my sternum, and finds its mark. My heart starts pounding, a ritual drum and a death knell all at once. Something above me, above the cabin, lurches and creaks. I hear the grind of metal on metal as my limbs start to tingle. Tears of joy and dread are already streaming down my cheeks. The lights flicker again as my back hits the cabin wall. For a moment, in the mirror, I see It. *I see It. So much bigger than it was before. So much closer.*

The lights go out again, leaving me in a little box of Nothing, and Its hand is around my throat.

I can no longer tell the difference between a scream and a moan.

Metal cables snap above us.

The air feels thicker. The Shadow surrounds me. Envelops me. I feel the pulsating chill of it on my skin. I am not certain whether it's found its way underneath my clothes, or whether it's somehow removed them altogether. *Absolved me of them.*

The Entity pushes closer. It traps me. The light flickers once more, and for the briefest blink of time, I peer into the endless dark of Its hood. Its gash mouth. Its endless tongue and endless teeth and *endless want for me hunger for me insatiable for me-*

"Please," I'm begging now. *"Please, please, take me, please- I'm yours, I'm yours- please-"*

A series of thick, metallic *snaps* go off like gunfire above my head. I gasp as the elevator shakes. Screeches. Plummets.

I am consumed.

—

Incident Report

Incident No: DB-00062
Date: ▓▓▓▓▓▓

CLIENT: ▓▓▓▓▓▓▓▓▓▓▓.

REPORTED BY: ▓▓▓▓▓▓▓▓▓

Description:

At approximately 08:42 AM, ▓▓▓▓▓▓▓▓▓▓
employee ▓▓▓▓▓▓▓▓▓ called Abram Murray Lifts to
report a stalled MRL elevator. Concerns were raised
regarding the repeat possibility of accidental
entrapment *(see Incident No. DB-00061)*. Elevator
Technician ▓▓▓▓▓ arrived on the premises at
approximately 08:58 AM. Upon arrival, Technician was
informed of alleged noises of distress heard inside the
elevator shortly after it was discovered stalled. Lift was
found to be nonresponsive. No emergency assistance
call was found to be made from inside the cabin. Power
to elevator was restored at approximately 09:36 AM.
Cabin was found to be empty upon inspection. Client
has requested replacement unit to avoid further
incidents.

Likely Cause of Incident: Faulty Equipment

Technician Recommendation: Unit Replacement

AML Representative Signature
Date ▓▓▓▓▓▓▓

Syren Nightshade *(she/her)* is a Canadian author, dancer, singer, actress, and performing artist. She has a long-standing love for Gothic horror and is incapable of keeping a short story short.

She wrote *tight.* while working in an overwhelmingly beige office building. She was deeply affected by the horror of the experience's mundanity.

She has never experienced sleep paralysis and hopes that she never will.

www.ingramcontent.com/pod-product-compliance
Lightning Source LLC
Chambersburg PA
CBHW030417120726
47904CB00007B/2310

9781068865039